THE FIVE LANDS

THE FIRE SHADOW

KONOHA NO KUNI
KONOHAGAKURE
NO SATO:

VILLAGE HIDDEN IN THE LEAVES

THE WATER SHADOW

KIRO NO KUNI
KIRIGAKURE
NO SATO:

VILLAGE HIDDEN IN THE MIST

THE LIGHTNING SHADOW

KUMO NO KUNI
KUMOGAKURE
NO SATO:

VILLAGE HIDDEN IN THE CLOUDS

THE WIND SHADOW

SUNA NO KUNI
SUNAGAKURE
NO SATO:

VILLAGE HIDDEN IN THE SAND

THE EARTH SHADOW

IWA NO KUNI
IWAGAKURE
NO SATO:

VILLAGE HIDDEN IN THE SHADOW

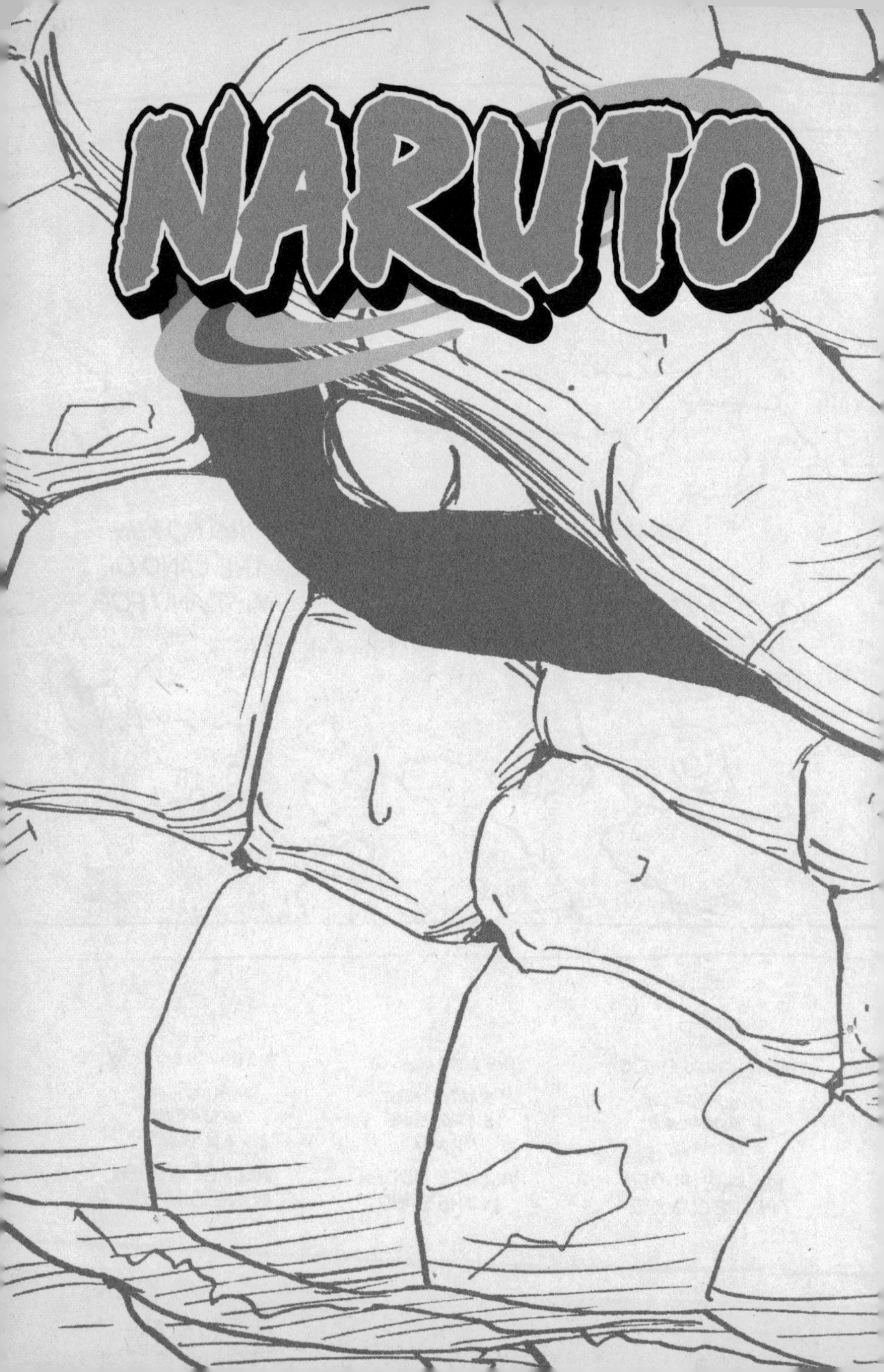
NARUTO

COWARD

ORIGINAL STORY BY MASASHI KISHIMOTO

ADAPTED BY TRACEY WEST

vizkids
VIZ MEDIA
SAN FRANCISCO

NARUTO COWARD
CHAPTER BOOK 12

Illustrations: Masashi Kishimoto
Design: Courtney Utt

Original manga first published in Japan in 1999 by SHUEISHA Inc., Tokyo.
This English language chapter book novelization is based on the original manga.

Published by VIZ Media, LLC
P.O. Box 77010
San Francisco, CA 94107

www.viz.com

West, Tracey, 1965-
Coward / original story by Masashi Kishimoto ; adapted by Tracey West.
p. cm. -- (Naruto ; 12)
"A VIZ kids book."
Summary: Part two of their final ninja examination takes Naruto and his teammates into the Forest of Death, where they face their scariest enemy yet.
ISBN 978-1-4215-3042-0
[1. Ninja--Fiction. 2. Examinations--Fiction. 3. Monsters--Fiction. 4. Japan--Fiction.] I. Kishimoto, Masashi, 1974- II. Title.
PZ7.W51937Pt 2010
[Fic]--dc22

2009026953

Printed in the U.S.A.
First printing, March 2010
Second printing, March 2010

THE STORY SO FAR

Twenty-six teams are competing in the exam to become journeymen ninja, or *chunin*. Squad Seven, made up of Naruto, Sasuke, and Sakura, has made the cut. Now it's time for the second part of the exam.

The exam leader, Lady Anko, has told them the rules. The goal is for all three team members to bring one heaven scroll and one earth scroll to the tower in the middle of the forest.

The catch is each team starting out will get only one of the scrolls. They'll have to steal the scroll they need from another team. That means that out of twenty-six teams, only thirteen will make it to the end. The mysterious forest is filled with all kinds of dangers. Getting to the tower won't be easy, but Naruto's going to become a chunin no matter what it takes!

Naruto
ナルト

Naruto is training to be a ninja. He's a bit of a clown. But deep down, he's serious about becoming the world's greatest shinobi!

Sakura
春野サクラ

Naruto and Sasuke's classmate. She has a crush on Sasuke, who ignores her. In return, she picks on Naruto, who has a crush on *her*.

Sasuke
うちはサスケ

The top student in Naruto's class and a member of the prestigious Uchiha clan.

"**PART TWO** of the chunin exam begins ***NOW!***" yelled Anko, the exam leader.

WHOOSH! WHOOSH! WHOOSH!

Twenty-six ninja teams raced through gates into the Forest of Death. Some ran across the mossy ground. Others took to the trees. They silently jumped from branch to branch.

Naruto, Sasuke, and Sakura were in another part of the forest.

"Did you guys hear someone scream?" asked pink-haired Sakura. She shivered.

"This place is creeping me out!"

Naruto shrugged. His bright orange pants and jacket stood out in the dark forest. So did the spiky yellow hair on top of his head. Naruto had blue eyes and strange, whisker-like marks on his cheeks. His right cheek was marred with a thin scratch he had got before the exam started. Anko had thrown a *kunai* right past his face when she got angry about his bragging.

"I'm telling you, Sakura, it's no big deal," he said. He stretched and walked a few steps away. “Uh, I gotta go to the bathroom.”

“Not in front of me, bozo. *I'm a lady!*” Sakura shrieked. “Use the bushes!”

She smacked him on the back of the head.

“Ow!” Naruto cried.

He walked off into the trees. He came back a few minutes later, grinning.

“Oh man, what a relief! I'm feelin' good

now," he bragged.

Sakura was annoyed. "Don't be gross!"

Sasuke studied Naruto carefully. His dark eyes narrowed.

POW!

Sasuke hit Naruto right in the face with a hard punch. Naruto flew backward, slamming into a tree. Sakura gasped.

"What the—?" she cried. "That was way over the top, Sasuke."

Naruto got to his feet. "What was that for?" he asked angrily.

"What have you done with Naruto?" Sasuke asked him.

Sakura was confused. "What?"

"Hello!" Naruto said, annoyed. "I'm right in front of you."

"The holder for your shuriken throwing stars is on your left leg, but Naruto is right-handed," Sasuke replied calmly. "And you forgot about the scratch on Naruto's cheek. You're even worse at disguise than the real Naruto."

POP! The ninja transformed back into his true form. He had wavy black hair. His ninja headband had four carved lines in it —the symbol of the Village Hidden in Rain.

He wore a white mask with holes cut into it over his eyes. Strangely, a metal plate was fitted over his mouth.

"Since you've forced me to come clean, why don't you do the same?" he asked. The metal plate changed the tone of his voice, making it low and hollow. "Which one of you has the scroll?"

SASUKE DIDN'T answer. He quickly threw a kunai at the ninja, who dodged it.

"Too bad. You've forced me to be direct," the ninja said.

He charged at Sasuke. Sasuke jumped up in the air. He pressed his palms together and swiftly made a series of ninja signs.

"Fire Style! Art of the Phoenix Flower! The Touch-Me-Not!" Sasuke cried.

WHOP! WHOP! WHOP! WHOP!

Sasuke shot four quick balls of fire from

his mouth. The ninja darted from side to side, narrowly missing each one. Then he jumped, landing on a low tree branch.

Sasuke chased after him. The boy hopped from branch to branch, going higher and higher each time. Sasuke was right on his heels.

Then he heard a shout from down below.

"**SASUKE!**"

Sasuke looked down. Naruto was tied up in ropes at the bottom of the tree.

That idiot! Sasuke thought. He tossed down a kunai so Naruto could free himself.

"Thanks!" Naruto called back.

The strange ninja swung back around and faced Sasuke. "You left an opening. Lucky me!"

WHIP! WHIP! WHIP! He sent three kunai slicing through the air. Sasuke ducked behind a thick tree branch. The kunai landed harmlessly in the wood.

Then he heard a strange sizzling sound. He peered underneath the branch. A piece of paper was attached to one of the throwing knives—and it was burning.

"A letter bomb!" Sasuke cried.

BOOM!

The bomb exploded, sending Sasuke flying

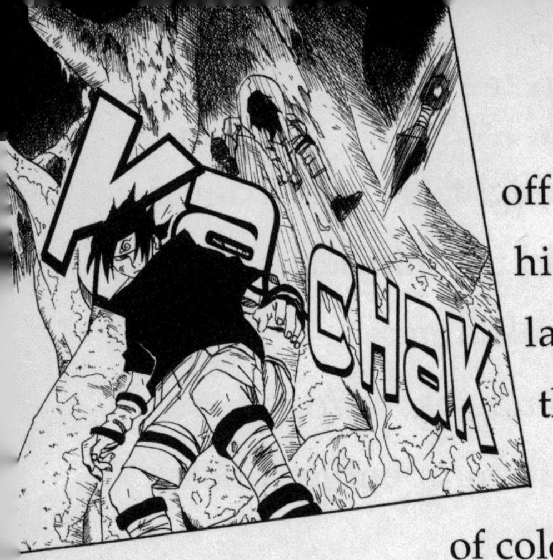

off the tree. He steadied himself in midair and landed on his feet on the ground below.

Then he felt the chill of cold steel on his neck.

"Better and better. One false move and I'll strike," the ninja said. "Now hand over the scroll."

The ninja just laughed—but then he turned as he heard a noise behind him. A kunai came flying through the air, aimed right for him. He jumped up into the trees to avoid it. Sasuke grinned.

It was Naruto!

"You're not getting away that easy!" Naruto yelled as he raced toward them.

Sasuke jumped up and threw a kunai toward the attacker. The knife sliced through the ninja's sleeve, pinning him to the tree.

The ninja pulled the kunai from his sleeve. With his last ounce of strength, he pushed himself away from Sasuke.

He quickly leapt off through the trees. Sasuke slumped to the ground, exhausted.

Naruto and Sakura gathered around him. They sat on the forest floor.

"Remember this, if we get separated," Sasuke said. "We have to be careful, or we could get tricked again."

"But what can we do?" Sakura asked.

"We need a secret password," Sasuke said. "That way, if one of us gets it wrong, we'll know it's an enemy impostor."

Sakura and Naruto nodded.

"Listen carefully," Sasuke said, lowering his voice. "I'll say it only once. Our password will be a poem called 'Ninki.' When I ask for it, here's what you respond...

"'We thrive in the chaos of the enemy tide. Quiet ninja don't need dens to hide,'" Sasuke said. "'Our only concern is to watch and wait, until the enemy lowers the gate.'"

"Bingo!" Sakura's eyes flashed. She had memorized it easily.

Naruto grimaced. "You expect me to remember that—**how?**" he complained.

"You are such a dunce," Sakura said. "I've already got it down!"

"We need a better password," Naruto was saying. "How about 'swordfish'?"

Sasuke stood up, sighing. "I'll take the scroll, Naruto."

SUDDENLY, NARUTO felt something small and sharp hit his cheek.

"**OW!**" Naruto cried, rubbing the spot. "What was—"

FWOOOOM!

A massive storm of wind and dust came roaring at them from the heart of the forest.

"A new enemy?" Sasuke cried.

The powerful winds surrounded them, slamming into their bodies. All three ninja jumped, seeking cover under the thick roots of the giant trees.

BOOM!

There was a huge explosion, then silence. The dusty storm died down. The force of the winds had dug a tunnel into the dirt, making a path through the forest.

At the start of the path stood three ninja wearing cone-shaped straw hats. The ninja with the dark hair, the one who had been hiding in the log, stood in the center of the team.

"Stick around, you two. It could be fun!" the ninja said. "I'll go alone."

Down the path, Sasuke hid under a leafy bush. He waited quietly for some sign of the attackers.

Then Sasuke heard a sound behind him.

He jumped up and whirled around. Sakura was hurrying toward him.

"Sakura," he said softly.

"Sasuke," she replied.

Sasuke held out his right hand. "Stay back! Don't come near," he urged. "What's the password? The 'Ninki'?"

"Oh, right," Sakura said. "'We thrive in the chaos of the enemy tide, quiet ninja don't

need dens to hide. Our o concern is to watch and wait, until the ene lowers the gate.'"

Sasuke nodded. "Good!"

Naruto ran up to them. "Yow! You guys all right?"

"Not so fast, Naruto," Sakura warned. "What's the password?"

Naruto smiled. "Right! 'Ninki,'" he began. '"We thrive in the chaos of the enemy tide, quiet ninja don't need dens to hide. Our only concern is to watch and wait, until the enemy lowers the gate.'"

Sakura sighed with relief. But Sasuke had a strange, dark grin on his face. He quickly pulled his arm back and hurled a kunai right at Naruto!

"HEY!" ...uto yelled. He jumped out of the way.

"Wha... Sakura was confused. She turned to Sasuke. "What are you doing? Naruto got the password *right*!"

"And this time, he's good enough to deflect my attack," Sasuke said. He kept his eyes on Naruto.

Sakura was angry. "Wait just a second here!" she yelled.

Naruto's eyes narrowed. He gave an evil-sounding chuckle.

"Heh. Well done!"

ONG!

A whirlwind surrounded Naruto. The wind died, and the ninja in the straw hat stood in his place. "What gave me away?"

Sasuke and Sakura both recognized the ninja with the long, creepy tongue.

"I knew someone was listening to everything we said," Sasuke explained. "That's why I chose that kind of password…the kind the real Naruto would never manage to memorize. Gotcha, impostor!"

"I see," the ninja replied, taking off the straw hat. "Watch and wait, eh? This is going to be more fun than I thought!"

The dust storm had blown Naruto all the way down to the end of the path. He lay flat on his back, his feet sticking straight up in the air. He slowly rolled over.

"**OW!**" he moaned. That wind had beaten

him up.

Raising his head, he saw the long dirt path the wind had made.

"Where did Sasuke and Sakura go?" he wondered.

He gazed around the forest. Then he noticed that an enormous shadow had fallen over him. He looked up.

His blood froze. A gigantic snake towered over him. A long black tongue dangled from the reptile's mouth.

"It's—**HUGE!**" Naruto screamed.

SSSS
...HUGE!!!

I'VE NEVER *seen a snake that big! W-what is up with this forest?*

The snake's eyes glowed as it targeted Naruto. Naruto snapped out of his fear just in time.

The snake quickly dove at Naruto. He jumped out of the way, avoiding the snake's huge head. *Slam!* The snake's head collided with the forest floor.

But before Naruto could run, the snake's long tail wrapped around his body. Naruto struggled to get free, but the tai him trapped in a tight grip.

The snake lifted Naruto up to its h mouth. It opened wide.

"**AAAAAAGH!**" Naruto screamed in terro as the snake swallowed him in one big gulp.

"Get me outta here!" Naruto wailed. Inside the snake's mouth felt gross and slimy. The snake slurped, and Naruto felt himself slide down the reptile's massive throat.

"Hey!" he yelled. "**IT ATE ME!**"

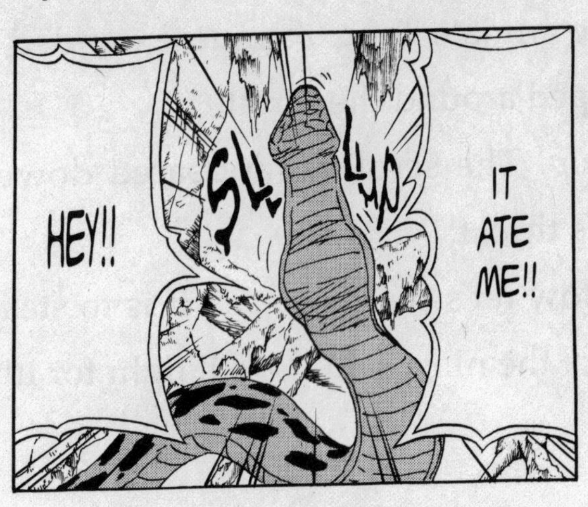

rby, Sakura and Sasuke were sizing up t' inja with the creepy tongue.

Sakura kept her eyes on the mysterious ninja. *This one gives me the creeps,* she thought. *Where is Naruto anyway?*

The ninja held up a scroll with the word *Earth* on the label.

"I suppose you'd like to steal our earth scroll, wouldn't you, since you've already got a heaven scroll," the ninja said smoothly.

Sakura and Sasuke watched, stunned, as the ninja's long tongue extended and wrapped around the scroll.

Gulp! The scroll disappeared down the ninja's throat.

"Now let's see how easy it is to steal my scroll," the ninja said. "We'll fight for it!"

The ninja's eyes seeme[illegible] penetrate through them. Sakura and S[illegible]ke felt a strange sensation at first. Then...

They fell to their knees as a wave of pain hit them both. Had they been attacked?

After the pain came something much worse—a feeling of pure terror. Sasuke had never felt anything like it in his life. The terrible feeli[illegible]wrapped around his brain like a slug.

It's [illegible] illusion, he thought. *We weren't attacked [illegible]it just felt like we were. The ninja has mad[illegible] us feel it and believe it. Who the heck are we dealing with?*

5

SASUKE GLANCED over at Sakura, hoping she had resisted the illusion somehow. But Sakura was on her knees, pale and shaking.

"Sakura?" Sasuke asked. But she didn't respond.

Crud! If we don't get out of here now, we're finished, Sasuke knew. But how could they run when they couldn't move?

"Heh," laughed the ninja. "I imagine you're

paralyzed by now."

Not quite, Sasuke thought. *I can move...just enough. We have to break the illusion.*

It took every ounce of strength he had, but he pulled back his arm and hit himself on the leg as hard as he could.

Nearby, Naruto was still struggling to get out of the snake's belly.

"**HEY, YOU!**" he yelled. "You better spit me out while you've got the chance!"

The snake's muscles were squeezing Naruto tighter and tighter. He couldn't move.

Rats! he thought. *I gotta get outta here before Mister Slimy digests me. But how do I make this freak barf?*

He thought about one time when he'd

been sick. He'd eaten bowl after bowl of his favorite dish, ramen noodles. He'd eaten so many bowls he couldn't count them all.

"That's it!" Naruto yelled. "Art of the Doppelganger! Solid Form!"

BAM! BAM! BAM! BAM! BAM!

Exact copies of Naruto popped into being, filling up the snake's belly. There were too many Narutos to count.

KA-BOOM!

The snake's belly exploded, spilling the army of slimy Narutos onto the forest floor.

The real Naruto stepped out from the crowd.

"I'm the ninja who'll become Lord Hokage, so don't mess with me," he bragged. "I've got better things to do with my life than to end up as a big piece of *snake poo.*" He brushed some snake slime off his orange jumpsuit.

"Right!" he said. "Now, to find Sakura and Sasuke."

Back under the tree, Sasuke's punch to his leg broke the illusion.

Sakura started, "Speak to me, Sas—"

Sasuke clapped a hand over her mouth before she could finish.

"We've got to move fast, or we'll be found," he whispered. "The question is how to escape. Um…how do we run? Um…"

Sasuke is so jumpy! Sakura thought. *I've never seen him like this.*

Sasuke peered around the tree trunk, looking for any sign of the strange ninja. He didn't notice the giant snake that lowered itself down from the tree branch above. Sakura peeled Sasuke's hand off of her mouth and screamed.

"**SASUKE! SNAAAAAKE!**"

The snake opened its mouth wide and lunged for them. Sasuke and Sakura each flew to one side. Sasuke propelled himself backwards.

The snake quickly wrapped itself around

and around the tree branch until it reached Sasuke. It opened its mouth again, revealing four sharp fangs.

For one second, Sasuke saw the face of the strange ninja in the face of the snake. He cried out in fear. Could the ninja and this monster be one and the same?

"*Yaaaaah!* ***GET LOST!***" he cried. He hurled every throwing star in his pocket at the snake.

WHOMP! The snake landed on the forest floor with a thud. Sasuke perched in a tree branch, panting.

Then Sasuke and Sakura both gasped. The snake's skin began to rip open. The dark-haired ninja climbed out of the snake's body!

"For shame, letting your guard down," the ninja taunted. "Stay on your toes, like a good ninja should. It makes the chase so much more rewarding...for the predator."

THE NINJA wound around the tree branch so fast that Sasuke thought his attacker was part snake. Sasuke froze in terror once more.

But before the ninja could attack, a storm of throwing stars landed in the tree above the ninja's head. Sasuke looked down. It was Naruto!

"Sorry, Sasuke," Naruto said. "I can't remember that stupid password!"

"***SWEET, NARUTO!***" Sakura cheered. "That was awesome!"

"Naruto to the rescue, huh?" Sasuke called down. "I know you're psyched to be saving the day, but now would be a good time to run for your life. This ninja is way out of our league!"

The ninja looked down at Naruto and laughed.

"Heh, heh. My compliments on your defeat of the giant snake, Naruto," the ninja hissed.

Naruto was surprised. *This ninja's a freak! I'll bet this creep is the one who sent that big snake to get me!*

Just thinking about it made Naruto angry. Farther up the tree, Sasuke was trying to figure out what to do.

"***HEY!***" Naruto shouted to their attacker. "Why don't you pick on someone your own size—or something like that..."

I've got to stop this before he gets us all killed, Sasuke realized.

He stood up and took the scroll from its hiding place on his body. Then he held it out.

"If it's our scroll you want, come and get it!" he yelled. "Just... **TAKE IT AND GO!**"

NARUTO WAS furious. "*WHAT?*" he yelled.

Sakura was wide-eyed with surprise. "Huh?"

The ninja smiled and gave a small chuckle.

Naruto pointed at his squad member. "Sasuke! What the heck do you think you're doing? Is this some clever way of beating the enemy? By handing over everything we've got?"

"Come and get it!" Sasuke shouted,

holding out the scroll.

Naruto couldn't believe it. Would Sasuke really give up their scroll to this monster? He watched, shocked, as Sasuke tossed the scroll to the snake ninja.

Naruto moved quickly. He jumped up, somersaulted, and grabbed the scroll in midair. He landed on the tree branch next to Sasuke.

"Stay out of this!" Sasuke shouted angrily. "You'll ruin everything!"

POW!

Naruto reeled back and hit Sasuke with a hard punch.

"Huh?" Sakura shouted.

Sasuke groaned. "What do you think you're doing?"

Naruto was on his feet, huffing and puffing.

"Naruto, what are you—" Sakura asked.

"I forgot the password, so I can't prove it, but this so-called Sasuke is obviously **A FAKE!**" Naruto said.

Sakura's eyes widened. "What?"

"Naruto, you idiot. I'm me!" Sasuke told him.

"That's a lie," Naruto replied. "And *you're* the idiot, idiot! You're a coward, which Sasuke is not. So you're not him! I'm not so sure we need to be afraid of this creep. And even if we did hand over the scroll, there's no

guarantee that we'd be spared."

The snake ninja smiled. "Naruto is right. Why bargain when I can simply kill you… and take the scroll?"

The ninja lifted up a sleeve to reveal a

strange tattoo on the left arm.

Naruto growled angrily. "Shut up!" he shouted. He jumped toward the ninja, ready to attack.

"Don't do it, Naruto!" Sasuke screamed.

The ninja began to perform a series of swift hand movements.

"The Art of Summoning!" the ninja cried.

A strong wind swirled around the ninja. Another giant snake appeared from within the wind. The ninja stood on the snake's head.

BAM!

The snake lashed out with its tail, snapping the tree branch underneath Naruto's feet. He plummeted down and then broke through the next branch.

"Naruto!" Sasuke and Sakura screamed.

Wham! Naruto landed with a thud on a thick branch.

"Excellent," the ninja said. "But let's not take any chances. Eat the boy!"

The snake's long, slimy tongue rolled out of its mouth. It plucked Naruto off the branch and wrapped around Naruto's body.

Then it slowly carried Naruto toward its wide, gaping mouth.

A STORM of rage welled up inside Naruto. When he was a baby, the spirit of the Nine-Tailed Fox Demon had been sealed inside his body to save his village. When Naruto got really angry, parts of the demon came out.

Like now.

Naruto's eyes burned red. His canine teeth turned into fangs. The whisker-like marks on his cheeks deepened.

"**EAT SNOT, SUCKER!**" Naruto yelled. He freed himself from the slimy tongue.

POW! POW! POW!

He punched the snake in the nose again and again.

For the first time, the snake ninja looked surprised. Sakura didn't know what to make of it either.

"Naruto's completely snapped, but... where did he get that kind of power?" she asked out loud.

The giant snake shook its head, sending Naruto tumbling to the ground. Naruto jumped back to his feet. He charged toward the snake.

WHOOSH!

The ninja shot a huge fireball at Naruto. The hot flames washed over his body. He let out an angry roar as he fell to the ground.

Is that really Naruto? Sasuke wondered.

"Ho, ho...and the fun has just begun!" said the snake ninja. "And it's Sasuke's turn next. How will he take it?"

The ninja turned and aimed the giant snake right at Sasuke. Sasuke stood, frozen in fear, as the snake prepared to pound him into the ground.

"**SASUKE!**" Sakura screamed.

Naruto had to save Sasuke from the giant snake. He threw himself against the snake to block him from reaching Sasuke. Naruto looked at his friend, and his eyes glowed red. "Hey, are you okay...you ***BIG CHICKEN!***"

Sasuke stared at Naruto. He remembered a time when he had said those exact words to his friend. He always gave Naruto a hard time. Now Naruto was turning the tables on him.

Sasuke felt lost and confused. The snake ninja had totally messed with his mind.

"***YAAAH!***" Naruto screamed. The snake

tongue wrapped around Naruto and dangled him in front of the snake ninja.

The snake ninja got close to Naruto's face. "Heh heh. The brat of Nine Tails is still alive and kicking," the ninja said. "How interesting. When he is angry, he loses himself, and a bit of the Demon Fox within comes through."

The ninja lifted up Naruto's orange jacket. "There's the proof. The spell that seals the monster within appears on your skin like a tattoo."

The ninja was right. A black spiral surrounded by sunburst lines covered Naruto's stomach.

The ninja made swift hand movements once more. Purple light glowed from each finger on the ninja's right hand.

"A five-pronged spell!" the ninja yelled.

Naruto cried out as the ninja's glowing hand hit his stomach.

"Sasuke! Naruto needs you!" Sakura yelled.

The red fire faded from Naruto's eyes. Whatever strength he had gained from the Demon Fox left him. He hung limply from the snake's tongue.

The Demon Fox has been trapped inside him for twelve years, the ninja thought. *But soon the energy of the boy and the energy of the demon will combine.*

The snake ninja took the heaven scroll from Naruto's pack.

"But today you are more trouble than you are worth."

The ninja nodded, and the giant snake tossed Naruto away with amazing force.

He's bound to fall! Sakura realized. She quickly threw a kunai at Naruto. It sliced through his shirt and pinned him safely to the tree branch.

"Sasuke!" Sakura screamed. Why wasn't Sasuke helping? "Naruto may be nothing like you. He's clumsy and he holds us back. And sometimes he's a pain, but at least he's got guts. Naruto's no coward. Right?"

Coward. The word stung Sasuke like a blow from a shuriken. He closed his eyes and remembered the last time he'd been called a coward.

His older brother towered over him.

"Baby brother, you're pathetic..." he had

said. "Hate me…and live like the coward you are. Cling to life without honor."

Sasuke opened his eyes. They were bright red and marked with the symbol of the Sharingan.

"***NO!***" Sasuke cried.

WHILE BATTLES raged on in the Forest of Death, three exam proctors made a terrible discovery outside the forest gates. Three students lay in the garden of stone Buddha statues.

"One, two, three," counted a proctor wearing glasses. "This is a very serious situation."

"The result of some kind of high-powered ninja skill," added the second.

The third proctor scratched his bushy-haired head. "Bad news, starting out with a problem like this." He nodded to the first proctor. "Report this to Lady Anko, who's in charge of the chunin exam."

"Yessir," the ninja replied.

Anko was sitting on top of the hut outside the gates of the Forest of Death. She was happily eating her lunch.

"Mmm, nothing goes better with rice dumplings than oshiruko bean soup," she said. She pulled one of the dumplings off of a wood skewer and washed it down with a gulp of soup. "As soon as I'm done, I'll get to the tower so I can greet any teams who have passed the test already. The good ones should be done in less than a day."

Suddenly, the proctor appeared in front of her.

"Terrible news, Lady Anko," he said.

"Something strange happened to three students."

"Three of them?"

"It's very serious...and very weird," the ninja told her. "Come and see for yourself."

Anko jumped off the hut and went to the garden with the proctor.

The bushy-haired proctor approached them.

"We checked their papers," he explained. "They were all from the Village Hidden in Grass. They were registered to take part in the chunin exam."

A cold shiver of fear passed through Anko's body.

No doubt about it. Now that I see them, I know whose technique was used here. But why would he meddle in this?

"Show me their photos," Anko said.

The proctor passed the photos to her. The first photo showed a ninja with long dark hair—the ninja with the snakelike tongue. Anko got a bad feeling in her gut. Everyone in the Forest of Death was in terrible danger.

"This is awful!" she cried. "You three!

Report what's happened to Lord Hokage. Ask that he send two Black Ops to the Forest of Death at once. I'm going after the impostors."

"HEH, HEH," laughed the snake ninja looking at Sasuke's eyes. "It looks like the blood of his ancestors is rising up in him."

The ninja made some swift hand motions. "We'll take our time, so you can show me all your moves!"

WHOOSH!

A small tornado of wind surrounded Sasuke. Another ninja would have been knocked down. But Sasuke stood firm.

He reached into his pack and pulled out

every weapon he had.

I've been living with the hope of one day taking down my older brother, he thought. *I thought it was the most important thing. But maybe I've been a fool all this time.*

He jumped high into the air, almost reaching the tops of the trees. His energy was strong.

Someone who can't even stand up and do what has to be done at a time like this wouldn't stand a chance in a fight against...him.

Sasuke dove down through the air, aiming right for the snake ninja.

The ninja dodged out of the way so fast Sasuke couldn't see the movement. He lunged at the snake ninja again, but he just couldn't catch up. WHOOSH! WHOOSH! WHOOSH!

The two ninja chased each other across the forest floor.

Sasuke focused his eyes on the snake ninja. If he concentrated hard enough, he could keep track of the ninja's movements. He thought quickly. Then he tied the end of a long roll of string to a kunai.

He chased after the snake ninja, throwing the kunai in the ninja's path every time the ninja made a turn. At first, the ninja didn't notice the string.

Then Sasuke threw the roll of string and the kunai at the same time. The string wrapped around the snake ninja, tightening around the ninja's body.

"He did it!" Sakura cheered.

Sasuke put his hands together, ready for a powerful ninjutsu move.

"Hah!" Sasuke said.

The snake ninja knew trouble was coming. *He means to use the Art of Dragon Flame!*

Sasuke released his hands. A sizzling wave of flame raced from his fingers, slamming into the snake ninja's face. The fireball exploded. But the snake ninja was still standing.

"Sasuke!" Sakura raced to her friend's side.

"Amazing, that one so young has mastered the power of the Sharingan Eye," the snake ninja said. "You are truly worthy of the Uchiha name."

Sasuke and Sakura gasped in horror. The snake ninja's face seemed to be melting away.

It didn't look real—more like some kind of mask.

"In fact, I believe I want you after all," the snake ninja said.

The ninja's voice had grown deeper. A new face began to appear underneath the melting face—the face of a man with green eyes.

The ninja broke free from the string. Stepping forward, he focused one green eye on Sasuke and Sakura. Once again, they were frozen to the spot. They couldn't move.

We're paralyzed, they both realized.

"Just who the heck are you?" Sasuke yelled angrily.

"I'm Orochimaru, the giant snake," the ninja replied. He held out the heaven scroll, which burned in his hands. "If you'd like a rematch, then pass this exam as quickly as you can."

Sakura gasped at the sight of the burning scroll.

"I'll see you again, if you manage to defeat the three ninja from the Village Hidden in Sound," Orochimaru promised. "They answer to me."

"What are you babbling about?" Sakura yelled. "We never want to see your face again!"

"Perhaps not," Orochimaru said. "But wishing won't chase me away."

The ninja's neck suddenly became long, like the body of a snake. Orochimaru reached out and sank his fangs into Sasuke's neck. Sakura watched, helpless.

Then Orochimaru returned his head to his body.

"I look forward to seeing you again, Sasuke," he said.

Sakura glanced at Sasuke's neck. A symbol had appeared there—three black teardrops, arranged in a circle.

Sasuke fell to his knees, doubled over in pain. "What's going on? Everything **HURTS!**"

Sakura turned to Orochimaru, angry. "What did you do to Sasuke?"

"Just a little something to remember me by," Orochimaru said. Then he sank into the dirt and disappeared.

Sasuke rolled on the ground, moaning in pain. Sakura didn't know what to do. She looked up into the tree. Naruto still hung there, unconscious.

Tears filled Sakura's eyes. She gripped

Sasuke in a hug, wishing she could take his pain away.

"Oh, Sasuke," she said softly. "W-what should I do?"

WH-WHAT SHOULD I DO...?!

Ninja Terms

Chunin

Chunin are ninja who are qualified to watch over and guide other ninja.

Genin

Genin are the lowest level of ninja. Genin are given headbands with their village's symbol on it to represent where they are from.

Jonin

Jonin are highly experienced ninja who serve as squad leaders.

Jutsu

Jutsu means arts or techniques. Sometimes referred to as *ninjutsu,* which means more specifically the jutsu of a ninja.

Kunai

A *kunai* is a small knife with a grip that can be used in combat.

About the Authors

Author/artist **Masashi Kishimoto** was born in 1974 in rural Okayama Prefecture, Japan. After spending time in art college, he won the Hop Step Award for new manga artists with his manga *Karakuri* (Mechanism). Kishimoto decided to base his next story on traditional Japanese culture. His first version of *Naruto*, drawn in 1997, was a one-shot story about fox spirits; his final version, which debuted in *Weekly Shonen Jump* in 1999, quickly became the most popular ninja manga in Japan. This book is based on that manga.

......

Tracey West is the author of more than 150 books for children and young adults, including the *Pixie Tricks* and *Scream Shop* series. An avid fan of cartoons, comic books, and manga, she has appeared on the New York Times Best Seller List as the author of the Pokémon chapter book adaptations. She currently lives with her family in New York State's Hudson Valley.

The Story of Naruto continues in: Chapter Book 13 *Beauty Is the Beast*

Naruto and the other boy ninja have all had their chance to be tough. Now it's the girls' turn! First, their teacher, Anko, steps in to help during a battle against Orochimaru, their weirdest enemy yet! And then Sakura must make a very big decision!

COLLECT THEM ALL!

#1 THE BOY NINJA

#2 THE TESTS OF A NINJA

#3 THE WORST JOB

#4 THE SECRET PLAN

#5 BRIDGE OF COURAGE

#6 SPEED

#7 THE NEXT LEVEL

#8 INTRUDERS

#9 THE CHALLENGERS

#10 THE FIRST TEST

#11 THE TENTH QUESTION

#12 COWARD

COMING SOON!

#13 BEAUTY IS THE BEAST